The Adventures of
Marco Flamingo
Under the Sea

Written and Illustrated by
Sheila Jarkins

To my husband, Gary ⋈ the catch of my life.

Text and Illustration © 2009 Jarkins, Sheila

All rights reserved. For information about permission to reproduce selections from this book,
write to: Permissions, Raven Tree Press, a Division of Delta Systems Co., Inc., 1400 Miller Parkway,
McHenry, IL 60050 www.raventreepress.com

Jarkins, Sheila

The Adventures of Marco Flamingo Under the Sea / written and illustrated by Sheila Jarkins;
– 1 ed. – McHenry, IL ; Raven Tree Press, 2009.

p. ; cm.

SUMMARY: The comical adventures of Marco continue as your favorite
flamingo explores the wonders of ocean life to find unlikely friends.

English Edition
ISBN 978-1-934960-68-4 hardcover

Bilingual Edition
ISBN 978-1-934960-66-0 hardcover
ISBN 978-1-934960-67-7 paperback

Audience: pre–K to 3rd grade.
Title available in English-only or bilingual English-Spanish editions.

1. Humorous Stories—Juvenile fiction. 2. Animals/Birds— Juvenile fiction.
I. Illust. Jarkins, Sheila. II. Title.

Library of Congress Control Number: 2009926215

Printed in Taiwan
10 9 8 7 6 5 4 3 2 1
First Edition

Raven Tree Press
A Division of Delta Systems Co., Inc.
www.raventreepress.com

Free activities for this book are available at www.raventreepress.com

"I played in the snow every day."

Marco was home at last. He was tickled pink to tell his friends about his latest adventure.

Marco was ready for another adventure. From his home in the calm lagoon, he saw the big waves of the ocean. That's where he wanted to go.

Marco was curious about the sea.
So he asked Manatee:
"What's under the water way out there?"

"It's no place for a flamingo,"
warned Manatee.

"Please tell me what you see
when you dive into the sea?"
Marco asked a flock of diving birds.

"It's no place for a flamingo,"
they warned.

Marco decided to find out for himself.
He plucked a reed and paddled out to sea.

Soon Marco came back. "I need something better than a reed," said Marco. "Wow. Snorkel gear. Thanks."

The snorkel gear worked better than the reed,
but Marco had to swim close to the surface.
That was a big problem.

He quickly found a solution.

When Marco got out to sea, he dove deeper and deeper.
Plop! Marco landed at the bottom of the sea.

Marco played all day—
at the top... at the bottom . . .
and at the places in between.

"Peek-a-boo.
I see you."

Marco raced a shark . . .

and sailed over the waves.

The seals invented a game
that they named after
their new friend.

"Marco!"

"Polo!"

23

That night, Marco slept under the stars.

In the morning, Marco sent
a message to his friends.

Dear Coral, Shelly, and Webb,
I love the ocean! I have had many adventures. I rode on a manta ray and raced a shark. My tank is empty so I'm heading home. See you soon.
Sincerely, Marco

P.S. I have a big surprise for you.

. . . Or could it?